the Shoe People

TRAMPY

by James Driscoll
Illustrated by Rob Lee

Storm Publishing

Trampy is a worn out boot.

When he was brought to the shoe mender's shop he was so worn out that he could not be mended. He had a big hole in his toecap and an even bigger one in his sole which let in water.

He looked extremely dirty and felt very sorry for himself.

In a corner of the shop was a large dustbin.

When Trampy heard the shoe mender say that it was impossible for the holes in his leather to be mended, he looked at the dustbin and thought to himself,

"Well, that looks like the end of me."

But Trampy was quite wrong.

The old shoe mender never threw any shoe or boot away. Instead, he polished Trampy's leather until it began to shine once more.

When the shoe mender had finished, Trampy looked quite smart for a worn out boot.

He put Trampy on a shelf in the back room of his shop. This was A VERY SPECIAL ROOM — a room with a secret.

Here, Trampy suddenly found himself in the Magic World of the Shoe People. He was very happy to be with so many new friends.

Trampy loves nature and especially likes to be in the countryside. He knows the names of nearly all the birds. He knows almost everything about wild flowers and trees.

The Shoe People, particularly Margot and Baby Bootee, love to go for long walks with him in the country. He tells them stories and makes everything sound so interesting.

Trampy lives in Shoe Street but is not very house proud.

He never paints his house so most of the paint has started to peel off. He never cleans his windows and never polishes his door knocker. There are some tiles missing from the roof and the chimney is very crooked, but Trampy doesn't attach much importance to houses.

He calls his house Tumbledown House.

The inside of Tumbledown House is always very untidy. Trampy simply hates tidying up.

The kitchen sink seems to be always full of dirty dishes. He doesn't like washing up either.

Trampy loves to sit in his favourite armchair in front of the fire and read his favourite newspaper, Shoe Town News.

Trampy is so kind and generous that everyone in Shoe Street loves him and no one minds his house being a little bit tumbledown.

No one that is, except Trampy's next door neighbour, Sergeant Major.

He objects particularly to Trampy's garden.

Trampy's garden is completely overgrown with long grass and lots of wild flowers.

There are buttercups, daisies, dandelions and two very big prickly blackberry bushes with the biggest, juiciest blackberries you have ever seen. Trampy can never bring himself to cut down the grass or the wild flowers because he loves them so much.

He knows that some of them grow over the fence into Sergeant Major's garden but that is just too bad for Sergeant Major.

Trampy has a table and some chairs in his garden.

He likes to sit at this table feeding and talking to his friends.

Trampy's friends are very special friends. They travel miles just to see him. Lots of birds and butterflies are always calling in. Even bees come to tea.

They all feel safe in Trampy's garden.

Trampy has two particularly close friends who call in to see him at least three times a week — a very prickly hedgehog called Hector and a bushy-tailed squirrel called Red. There is always a bowl of milk for Hector and a handful of nuts for Red on Trampy's table.

Trampy loves seeing his friends from the countryside.

Trampy often recalls the days when he was a smart new boot but feels that living in Shoe Town with the Shoe People are the happiest days of all.

If you were to ask him if he would like to return to the old days, he would say, "No thank you. I am very happy here in Shoe Town being just . . .

TRAMPY!"